To Katelyn,

2017

This one is for my children, Wyeth and Sadie.
I love you both more than you can know. I am so proud to be your Dad.

— J. L. M.

For Mom,

— K. V.

To Walter, Bobby, and Jason,
the best roommates I could ever ask for!

— V. K.

Acknowledgments

I owe an extraordinary debt to my wife, Jocie, who has offered her support and faith from the first day we met. Without her, this book certainly would not exist. I love you and appreciate all that you do for our children and me!

I would like to pay a special thanks to Mom and Dad.
Their dedication, kindness and love through the years have made it possible for me to become the person I am.

Thanks also to Vuthy Kuon who has given generously of his time and expertise for several years now to get this project completed.

Finally, thanks to all the kids, parents, librarians and teachers who have supported my work through the years and encouraged me with your kind words and smiling faces!

— *Lucas*

Published by Providence Publishing

(713) 480-7069

Printed in China through Morris Press Ltd

Sixth Printing 10 9 8 7

Library of Congress Catalog Card Number 2002108931

Fifi the Ferocious / Lucas Miller / Kenneth Vincent / Vuthy Kuon

Summary: Fifi the dog learns about nature, her animal friends, and their special gifts.

ISBN 978-0-9651661-6-4

Fifi
the Ferocious

story by
lucas miller

pictures by
kenneth vincent

produced by
vuthy kuon

PROVIDENCE PUBLISHING COMPANY
Houston

Behold . . . Fifi!
Fifi the Ferocious!
Isn't she . . . bold?
Doesn't she look . . . fearsome?

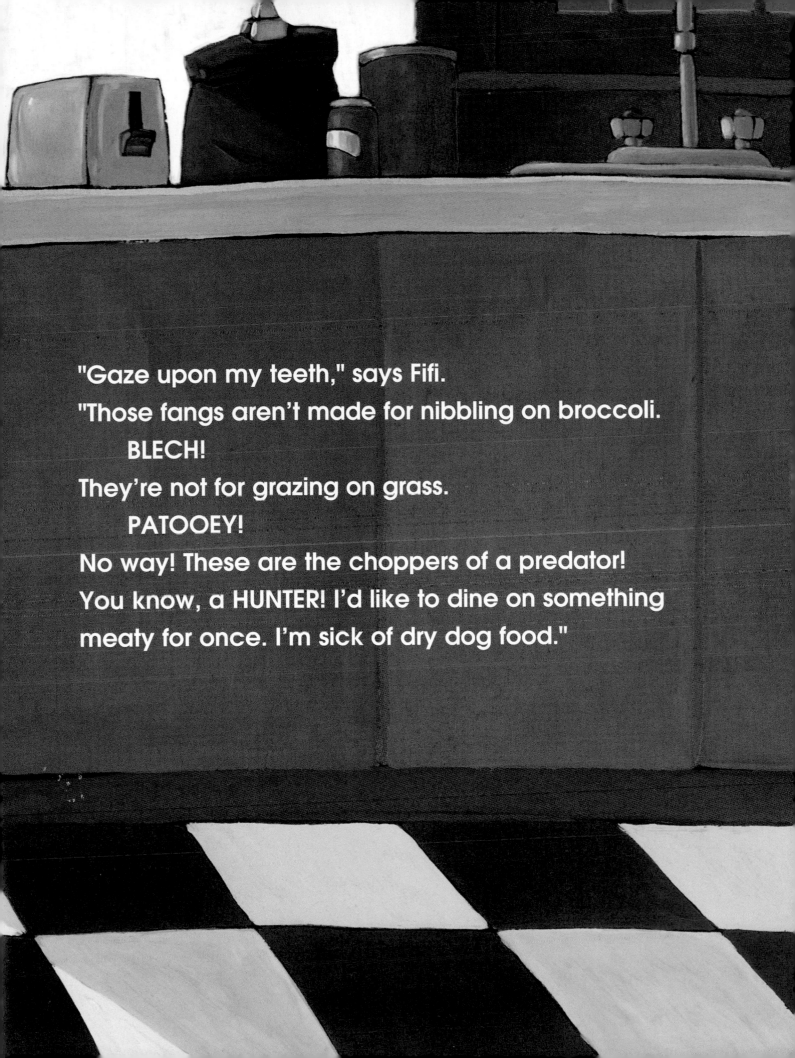

"Gaze upon my teeth," says Fifi.
"Those fangs aren't made for nibbling on broccoli.
　　BLECH!
They're not for grazing on grass.
　　PATOOEY!
No way! These are the choppers of a predator!
You know, a HUNTER! I'd like to dine on something
meaty for once. I'm sick of dry dog food."

But what's this? As Fifi surveys her kingdom, she discovers that her human left for work and didn't close the door all the way. Her chance to prowl and hunt has arrived!

Boldly, she strides through the doorway and into the wild, wild world beyond her cozy home.

"Hark!" she declares. "My first victim approaches! He's gonna be easy to catch, too, because he is so S-L-O-W!" What animal could it be?

A TURTLE!!!

"I may be slow," says the turtle, "but that's okay. I don't need to run away! I've got a hard shell made of bone and covered with tough, scaly skin. If that little lapdog tries to bite me, she's just going to hurt her teeth!"

Sure enough, Fifi pounces. She springs up high in the air and chomps down hard on that turtle's shell with all her might!

CRACK!!!

"OUCH!" she cries, "Somebody better call the doggie dentist!"

WHOOOOOSH!!!

The turtle tucks his head inside his shell in a flash! Instead of a mouthful of turtle, Fifi ends up with a mouthful of dirt!

"Hey, where'd his head go?" asks Fifi.

Still hungry, Fifi is soon back on the prowl. "I think I'd better look for something nice and soft this time! Here comes a tasty looking morsel! It looks fluffy, too!" Who could it be?

A SKUNK!

"Don't mess with me, ya' little puff-ball!" warns the skunk.

"And why not?" asks Fifi.

"Because if you try I'll just scare you away, I'll lift up my tail like this!" the skunk announces and raises his black and white backside high in the air.

"Oooh, I'm sooo scared!" mocks Fifi sarcastically.

"I warned you," the skunk snarls. "Now look out because here comes a dose of my finest skunk perfume!"

PSSSSSSHHHHH!!!!!

"Aye, Chihuahua!" says Fifi, holding her nose.
"You smell terrible!"

Fifi is still hungry and soon she's back on the trail. "I'm going to find a prey that's not so STINKY this time! Aha! I spy someone who's not so stinky! He doesn't have a bony shell either!" Without a second thought, Fifi hops up high and lands firmly upon a . . . PORCUPINE!

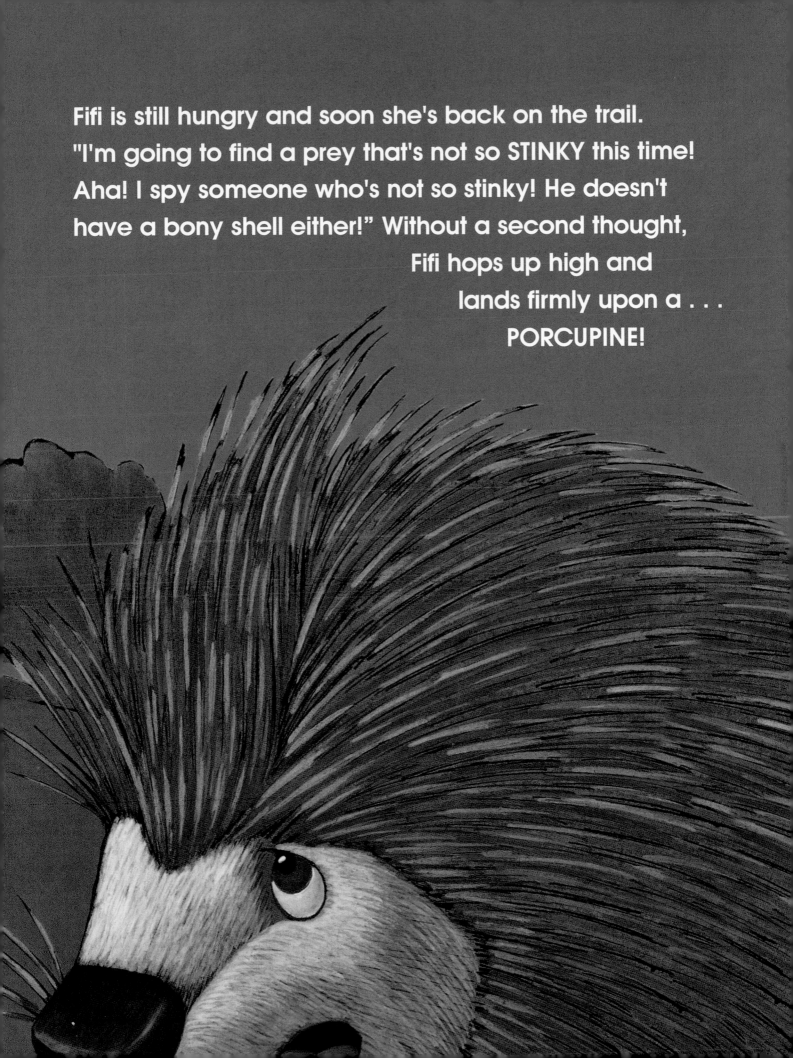

"Behold Fifi now!" says the turtle.
"Fifi the STINKY!" says the skunk.
"I think she's ready to go home!"
says the porcupine.

Poor Fifi! Her teeth ache from chomping down on the turtle's shell. She smells like the goo at the bottom of a dumpster behind a school cafeteria! And with porcupine quills still stuck in her snout, she just has to smile and say . . .

It 's not easy being a predator!

Author's Note

When I was about five years old, I discovered a box turtle crawling under my neighbor's bushes. (Five-year-olds love their neighbors' bushes, you know.) I was, to put it mildly, delighted, enthralled and amazed with that little turtle. Animals became a life-long interest for me and today I travel the nation teaching about wildlife with my songs and stories.

One of my most popular songs, "Laugh Ourselves Silly," is about the ways animals protect themselves from predators. I created a puppet play to introduce the tune, which took on a life of its own and became one of the highlights of my performances. That puppet play was the natural choice for this, my first full-length children's book. I am very pleased to share with you *Fifi the Ferocious*!

I know Fifi's antics will give you a laugh and I hope you will also learn a little about the ways animals protect themselves. I have found that blending science with music, stories and good-old silliness can make learning a joyful experience!

By the way, if you would like to hear "Laugh Ourselves Silly" you can listen to a sample at www.lucasmiller.net, or find it on my CD, *There's a Chicken on My Head!* You may also reach me at (800) 755-4415. I'd love to hear from you!

—Lucas Miller